Fences

and Other Stories

PHYLLIS A. DUNCAN

DEDICATION

To Vera McInnes, a teach who first told me it was all right to imagine other worlds and places and to write what was in my heart. I wish she could be here to see what that encouragement wrought.

For the children, nieces, and nephews of my heart and theirs.

CONTENTS

ACKNOWLEDGEMENTS

I'd like to acknowledge my family for providing the stuff of which stories are told and the family legends passed along—which I've embellished.

My thanks to friends, neighbors, teachers, professors, former students, and co-workers for their love, support, forbearance, and encouragement.

My gratitude to my writer friends from SWAG Writers, James River Writers, WriterHouse, Blue Ridge Writers, and the best indie fiction magazine around, *eFiction*, for giving me a chance. Thanks to Jennie Coughlin for the suggestion of re-doing *Rarely Well-Behaved* as more than one ebook.

CHOICES

I have no pictures of my grandmother as a child or a young woman. My favorite is one taken in her early years as a matron. She was in her late thirties, certainly no older than her early forties. It is a formal pose. Her hair is in a chignon but wavy around her face; she is unsmiling. That is the only hint she had endured a brutal marriage and buried an infant son.

In my memory, though, she is ever-smiling as she talked about her "babies," the ones she gave birth to and the ones she mid-wifed into this world.

That picture also doesn't show the choices she had to make, choices she began to make early in her life. Some she made freely, of her own accord. Others came from necessity, which begs the question: Can a choice made from necessity really be a choice?

My grandfather was one of those necessary choices. I know so little of him. His name was not to be uttered in front of my grandmother or my mother, his daughter. My uncle, his namesake and physical double, provided a few details, though nothing more, out of deference to his mother and sister.

This near-stranger whose genes I carry is a virtual unknown, and all I do know is that his family and my great-grandfather decided he and my grandmother should marry. He was thirty-four; my grandmother was seventeen and already qualified as a nurse, serious enough at that age, it was thought she would be a settling—

1

more like sobering—influence on him. She made that choice so she wouldn't disappoint her father. In the 1920's there was little else she could do.

The reality was she had tired of raising her full and half-siblings. Her marriage would be an escape from that drudgery, but the lesson from that was she could efficiently manage a household and bring in extra money with her nursing.

The attempts at stabilizing my grandfather were not as successful. The drinking increased, followed, inevitably, by battering. When she caught a fever from a patient and began to lose her hearing, my grandfather wouldn't let her tell anyone she could barely hear. If people knew she was going deaf, they wouldn't hire her. Her nursing was now their only source of income. His profession had become spending his time and her money in the local public house.

In time, they had a son, dutifully named after his father, and a daughter. My grandmother named her after the mother she'd lost at six. A second son died of pneumonia after my grandfather drank away the money intended to buy the winter's coal.

To his credit (and he gets so little), he was shamed into trying a new start. Friendship was the bit of luck that gave my grandmother a choice in how to begin again. A widowed friend now lived in America, and both sides of the family packed up and "came over on the boat" in the late 1920's, so she could have familiar company in her widowhood. (The twist is that beneficent widow was my paternal grandmother.)

My grandfather's new start was short-lived. My grandmother, now almost fully deaf, had learned to lip read and could hide that fact. As my grandfather got fired from menial job after menial job, she made another choice.

She knew one of the two local doctors performed illegal abortions, a chancy venture at the time. A doctor caught performing abortions then lost his license and faced prison time. (Now, they face harassment and death at the hand of so-called pro-lifers, so not much changed there.) The money she knew he made from the procedure appealed to her. She had two young children to feed, clothe, and house—and an alcoholic husband to keep in "the drink."

She made the doctor an attractive offer—train her, give her the proper instruments and medications, and she'd perform the abortions for him; then, they would split the fees—sixty percent for him, forty for her. He agreed but told her if she were caught he'd deny he knew anything about it.

That was an easy choice. She needed the money. Then, she chose to help rural and small-town women end unwanted or dangerous pregnancies. Because she'd been a Protestant in Ireland, she didn't eschew the training on methods of birth control, and she gave instruction on that—also illegal in Virginia then.

This was a profession, much like my hapless grandfather, never discussed in the family, and she only confided in me not long after the Roe v. Wade Supreme Court decision. She didn't really see what all the fuss was about. She believed a woman should decide when or whether to give birth. She wanted me and others to have the choices she didn't.

"And the money wasn't bad, either," she said.

The rich and poor women in her area came to her in distress and left less so. She took the money and didn't judge. That wasn't her place, she said. But when my now-married mother came to her for an abortion because she didn't want to share her husband with anyone, my grandmother refused.

My mother's subsequent self-abortion attempts—Lysol douches, pitching herself down a flight of stairs—weren't successful, and I'm still stubborn and pro-choice.

My grandmother kept up this distaff profession until a few years before she died. She never lost a single mother, and many of them returned to her for midwifery during their wanted pregnancies. Some, then and now, would call her a murderer. Most of her patients thought of her as a savior. She considered herself neither. She offered what she had rarely been able to take advantage of herself—choice.

I believe her final choice came on the night she died.

She was in robust health for seventy—a touch of arthritis, occasional aches and pains, mild high blood pressure. After the death of her beloved second husband on December 22, 1951, she would often declare, "I just want to go to sleep one night and not wake up."

3

On December 22, 1973, Maggie Marie Brown Pierce Smith chose to do just that.

GOING HOME

The young man was determined. The purposefulness of his stride, the set of his brow evinced that. He had walked nearly nine miles in the dark on cattle paths and over fences. He had ten more miles to go. Ten miles, and a man would die.

The young man—a boy of fifteen, really—had walked for more than two hours. He figured in two and a half or three more, he would reach his mother's house, his dead father's house, where his stepfather was. By midnight, then, he would be there. Soon after midnight, his stepfather would be dead.

Long walks can give one time to think, to reconsider. Hot heads have cooled in the time taken to reach the object of one's anger. Not this boy. Perhaps the Ulster Scot stubbornness was to blame, but his anger had abated none during his trek. It raged as much as it had when he overheard his oldest brother tell the tale. Their drunken stepfather had struck their mother for her failure to get dinner before him as quickly as he though she should. No one had seen the boy listening, and no one had seen him take the rifle from its rack or the ammunition from a shelf.

If I had been there, he thought, I would have stopped the bastard.

But he wasn't there. None of his nine siblings were there, either. The older ones were married and starting families of their own, but

5

the younger ones, the boy included, their mother had put out to relatives when their stepfather demanded it.

"By God, this is my house now!" All the children had cowered in the hallway to listen to his rage. "Only my children will live in this house. None of your brats with their high and mighty airs. You're just a farmer's wife now. Get them out."

At twelve, the boy had left only the second home he'd ever known.

He barely remembered the first, and his siblings said he shouldn't be able to remember at all. A few weeks past two years old and still in baby dresses, his own father died of a stroke. The boy swore he could remember being held by the man who was seventy when his youngest son was born. He could remember the crying and wailing afterwards and being tied in his crib to keep him from following the cars for the funeral.

A year later, when his mother married his coarse stepfather, most thought he was young enough to think of that man as his father. But he never did. He never would. He kept the scant memories of his own father close, as a comfort when he needed it. He needed that comfort a lot.

"I'm not that man's son" became a mantra, thought often enough, but said at inopportune times.

When he'd been forced from his home at twelve, he had looked to his mother, expecting her to say something, to tell him and his siblings to just go through the motions until the drunk slept it off. But she said nothing, did nothing to stop them from leaving. Her face had no expression, and only in later years did he realize there was emotion there—relief.

Every day of his three-year exile, the boy had expected his mother to come and bring him home, but none of the children could even enter the yard. They would stand outside the fence, and their mother would query them about homework and ask about behavior. She never answered the question, whether spoken or not: When can we come home?

The boy reached the crest of a hill overlooking his mother's house, his father's house, his home. He paused only to catch his breath and to calm the frantic beating of his heart. His hands couldn't shake and spoil his aim when he pulled the trigger.

In the white farmhouse, a light shone in one window in the parlor. His stepfather would be sitting there, drinking still, since the light was on. The boy's mother would be there, too. She couldn't rest until her husband passed out and she carried him to bed.

A voice in the young man's head, sounding like a teacher he admired, told him he was about to shoot a drunken man.

The boy shook his head. "No, I'm about to shoot a drunken son of a bitch."

His breathing and heartbeat normal, the boy inhaled a deep breath and released it, renewing his purpose, and strode down the hill to the farmhouse's front door. He didn't remember entering the house until he stood in the parlor in the rear of the house and saw what he knew he would see.

His stepfather sat in a battered armchair. A bottle of whiskey with a dram left sat on a table beside the chair. He clutched a glass in a beefy hand, his round face flushed, gray eyes bloodshot and bleary. He blinked several times when the boy entered, as if he didn't recognize him.

When the boy brought the rifle to his shoulder, the man became half-sober and laughed.

"Well, boy, you gonna shoot me?"

The boy didn't answer but laid his cheek against the rifle stock, aiming down the barrel as his oldest brother had taught him.

"You don't have the balls, boy. I ain't afraid of you."

Don't answer. Don't talk. Get it done.

"Go ahead, boy. Shoot. Did you remember to load it?" The laughter came again, and the boy focused on the bead at the end of the barrel, "setting" it in the notch in the sights. His stepfather's fleshy bulk was blurred beyond the barrel, and the boy's finger moved to the trigger, the first joint of his index finger slipping easily around it.

He took a deep breath and held it. Squeeze, don't pull, the trigger. His finger began to tighten.

The hazy image of his stepfather disappeared, replaced by the faded print of a woman's dress. The boy looked up. Between him and his target stood his mother. The right side of her face showed a miserable bruise; one cut, swollen lip distorted her voice.

"Move, Mother."

7

"No, son. I can't let you do it."

"Then, leave the room."

"And get what? A dead husband and a son in the electric chair? Put the gun down, son."

The gun slid from his shoulder to hang, useless, in his hands. He stopped fighting the tears he'd held inside for three years and wept. "Why, Mother, why?"

"I was a young woman married to an old man. Now, I'm married to a man my own age. You're too young to understand what that means."

"Come away with me, please."

She tried to smile, but her split lip made it too painful. "I'm this man's wife. My place is here, and you have your whole life ahead of you. You can't end it here."

"I'll only end his."

"The law won't see it that way. The state will wait until you're eighteen and execute you for killing an unarmed drunk in his own house. I want you to know your wife and hold your children."

His anger fueled by that he said, "At least I won't make my children leave their home."

The woman stared at him, not like a mother at all.

"You need to understand I love him. You kill him, you kill me."

The tears came again as the boy shook his head to deny all of it. The rifle clattered to the floor, and the boy fled the house he no longer wanted to be in. The last thing he heard before he stepped out into the cool night was his stepfather's laughter.

Forty years later when the life the boy took was his own, no one knew why.

FENCES

The woman clutched a picket on the white fence, planted her feet, and hauled backward, applying the considerable strength of her 180 pounds. Wood splintered and shards flew; nails at first held then released with a rusty screech. The picket came free.

Through the sweat and the strands of hair hanging in her face, she grinned with pure pleasure. Without looking, she tossed the plank over her shoulder. It landed amid the embers of its companions and began to burn.

When the pickets were all done and smoldering, she worked away at the horizontal supports until they, too, succumbed to the fire, their protest in the sharp pops and cracks as the paint bubbled and long-buried pockets of resin exploded in the heat. Only the sturdy posts remained.

The woman strode with intent toward the first in the line of posts. She embraced it like a lover and began to rock back and forth. By the force of her will and the strength of her determination, she loosened the dirt that had held it in place for decades. She squatted, gripped tighter, and heaved upward, pulling the post from the ground. One by one, the posts joined the fire, a blaze now whose smoke boiled skyward.

Breathing hard, dirty, and disheveled, the woman watched the smoke ascend until it met moving air aloft and trailed away. She walked past where the fence had been, up the brick walkway, and into her house.

* * *

The white fence had surrounded the farmhouse for almost 200 years. Family legend said when that fence—built by William Donaghy in 1749 around a plot where he'd yet to build a house for an as yet unknown bride—came down, the family would, too. The fence had survived wind and rain, been unscathed by a fire that destroyed Donaghy's first farmhouse, and been ignored by scavenging troops during the War Between the States.

Over the generations of its existence, the clean, white fence was the symbol of all the Donaghy's had and others didn't. In the midst of the Depression when houses and fences fell to ruin, only the Donaghy's could afford a groundskeeper whose sole responsibility was to check the fence's integrity, replace damaged boards, and apply a new coat of bright, white paint every spring and fall. As other farmers lost their land and homes to the banks and moved to town to join breadlines, that fence mocked their passage.

* * *

After soaking her aching muscles in a hot bath, the woman looked out the window of her second-floor bedroom. Though the fire still smoldered, she looked past it to the empty holes where the fence posts had been. Her husband and his family would be angry she'd dared to take the damned fence down. They couldn't understand her need to mark this house, one she cleaned, cooked in, and fucked her husband in, as her own.

Maeve Donaghy had married well and above her station, and she should be grateful they took pity on her, her in-laws said. Life within that family had absorbed her until little was seen or known of her except the name she took upon her marriage.

* * *

Maeve had first seen the fence, bright and glaring in the autumn sun, on the day her father took her out of school at thirteen to work with the rest of her family harvesting other people's crops. An intelligent, quiet girl, she loved animals, loved nursing their hurts, and had an unvoiced dream of being a veterinarian, but she never entered another classroom.

After she left school, every day for weeks, Maeve walked past that fence and the house it enclosed on her way to and from field work. She came to hate the Donaghy girls who peeked at her from behind lace curtains and laughed. Warm and smug in their fine, large house, the Donaghy girls didn't wear ill-fitting, hand-me-down clothes, didn't get their hands so dirty they never came clean, didn't walk inside a dirt-floor house and get chicken shit between their toes. The Donaghy girls had the ability to choose; Maeve didn't. The Donaghy girls chose what to wear, where to go, who to see, what to do. Maeve could only do what she was told—by her father now, by a husband someday.

The white fence's pickets mocked her the day her father walked her to the front door of the Donaghy house, barefoot, in a dress made from flour sacks, and pregnant. As her father demanded justice from the Donaghys' oldest son, Maeve glanced over her shoulder, out the sitting room window. The fence looked like sharp teeth in a maw ready to devour her.

She wanted to tell her father it was someone else, but before she could Donald Donaghy said, "It's all right. I'll do what's right by her."

Maeve shuddered as the fence snapped closed on her, shutting her inside the house she would come to hate even more. She felt a quiver somewhere behind her navel. Her reprisal—the child not quite real to her—had moved.

Months later, when Maeve lay in her childbed, sweating, exhausted, pained, and straining, the fence moved inside and stabbed her in her contractions. Then, the labor ended, and the midwife forced the "reprisal" into her arms. Maeve looked at the fine, wispy hair and into the trusting eyes and saw the realness of the child. She loved and knew love for the first time.

"James," she said. "But I'll call you Jimmy."

By the time Jimmy was four, the fence enclosed him and three siblings, but Maeve had learned to ignore it. She had to. It took all her strength to endure living in this family. The fence was always there but not as important as cooking, cleaning house, minding children, and satisfying a husband's needs.

* * *

A few months after the birth of her last child, Maeve realized she was pregnant again, the fifth time in as many years. She contemplated this while she sat at the vanity in her bedroom. She stared into the mirror and realized she was fading. She could see through herself the wallpaper and the fence from the window. Soon, she'd be completely gone.

That was acceptance, not fear. No one noticed her anyway. She was a nonentity, someone referred to not by her name but simply as Don's wife, another of his possessions.

Maeve tried to will herself back into existence but couldn't. In this house she was nothing. There was nothing of hers, not even her clothes, as she was constantly reminded, not even her children. They were ever referred to as "Don's children." She couldn't arrange the furniture to her own liking.

So she wouldn't have to see herself disappear, Maeve rose and went to the bedside phone. The call to the midwife—who also did things you didn't talk about—was brief, and they settled on a price. For Maeve any price was reasonable. She left the house, walked past the fence to her car. If she looked back she would see the fence snaking after her, ready to snatch her back.

She kept her eyes ahead.

* * *

Maeve lay on clean, white sheets spread over the midwife's kitchen table. Did her family eat here, Maeve wondered, after the midwife did her work? She kept her eyes on the ceiling, casting her thoughts far away from the tiny kitchen. A twinge in her womb made her flinch. The midwife patted Maeve's thigh to comfort her.

"It's all right. It'll only be a minute," the midwife said.

Soon, the pain, much less than childbirth, eased, and Maeve's hands began to tingle. She held them before her eyes. They seemed denser, more solid. Color and flesh formed and filled in the outlines. As the midwife scraped life out of her, Maeve substantiated.

The midwife folded a large towel over something. "I'm done." Without another word, she left Maeve alone with sanitary napkins and her clothes.

As she redressed, Maeve refused the tears that tried to fall, and she watched the rest of her become solid again. She lay four twenty dollar bills on the makeshift operating table and left for home.

When Maeve re-entered the yard and stood by the fence, she looked down at herself and saw she began to fade again. The fence was more real than ever, whiter than ever as it drained her. If she were not free of it, her molecules would scatter like smoke in a good breeze.

She ignored the midwife's cautions about rest and blood loss. She dropped her purse, kicked off her shoes, and reached for the first picket.

* * *

Maeve prepared herself for her husband's reaction when he returned from a business trip and saw the pile of charcoal and the flowers planted in the post holes. She stood smiling, her new self hard and resolved, and faced him as a person when he raged into the house. He lifted a fist to strike her for the first time ever, but on sight of her, his anger faltered. He sank into a chair beneath her incessant smile then grew silent and cold.

Maeve laughed then with a joy so profound it surpassed any physical pleasure she had ever known. The fence was gone, and Maeve moved, free, though the house, her house. The smile stayed as she touched a chair, adjusted the drapes, her hands casual in a caress of ownership. The smile was serene, ephemeral, and, best of all, would annoy her husband and his family. She would smile when she allowed them into her house and when she saw their reaction to what her husband had become—was he fading a bit now? Her smile grew broader.

They will fall, they will all fall, and I will live here in my house, on my land. And her smile didn't falter.

* * *

On Sunday, as was the custom, the family came for dinner after church. A smiling Maeve greeted them from where the fence used to be. They accepted the unaccustomed hugs and kisses from her, speechless from her transformation. Inside, her husband sat in a darkened room and smoked. He didn't respond to their calls to him.

All day, her house abounded with nieces and nephews playing games with her children. Maeve smiled all through dinner, even though her mother-in-law complained about the rearranged furniture. She smiled when she overheard her sisters-in-law comment about her weight and her clothes. She smiled when her brothers-in-law complained the meat was overdone. After dinner, she smiled when she sent the children out to play in a yard with no fence.

Let them see it was only a fence. Let them see this is all mine now.

She smiled through the screams.

She smiled when her husband carried in a bundle of filthy, bloody rags and laid it on her clean, kitchen table. Her husband shouted for quiet. Someone whispered that they needed to call for the doctor.

"It's too late for a doctor," her husband said. The house fell silent in finality.

Maeve's husband turned to her with an expression she would see for the rest of his life—pain and hate and fear and desperation in a single glance. His eyes drew hers to the thing on the table.

Eyes that had looked at her with trust at his birth were open, vacant, filmed like those of a fish too long out of water. Her smile became a rictus.

Maeve thought it was a bundle of rags because the clothes she'd dressed him in that morning were shredded. His face was raw flesh, skin hanging in tatters. The missing fence, which had made her whole, freed Jimmy to run onto the gravel road and into the path of a car. The car dragged him a quarter mile before the horrified driver could stop.

* * *

People would say of her, "She bore up well during the wake and the funeral."

As relatives sobbed and keened around the gravesite, Maeve looked down at her legs where she sat. She was more solid, more substantial, more real than she'd ever been. When she saw that, the smile returned, small and wan and mad.

When the last clot of dirt dropped on the coffin, Maeve put all thought and knowledge of the child away. She required the same of everyone else. His name would not be spoken in her presence, could never be used by anyone to name another child. He never existed.

For years afterward, whenever Maeve looked out any door, any window, she saw a new fence growing. This time, hard, black iron budded from where her flowers had bloomed. It took fifty years to finish growing, but it kept out everything and everyone, except the few she allowed.

14

Maeve was right. She did outlast them all and died in her bed in her house on her land, surrounded by her fence, alone.

WHAT'S IN A NAME?

State Senator Nancy Dale looked at me over her half glasses. "You expect me to read this before the press?"

"It's the truth," I said.

"The 'truth' of a bunch of convicts."

"Convicts can't tell the truth?"

"Annie, pull in your liberal claws. They will say anything they think will get them outta jail."

"Before they've paid their debt to society?"

"Exactly."

"Senator, this is a minimum security prison. No armed robbers or murderers. Just bad-check writers and shoplifters."

"Shoplifters are thieves, you know."

"Nancy, my Aunt Margery, the quintessential Southern belle, got caught about once a month lifting lace hankies from Newberry's. Do you think she spent any time in the Culpeper County Jail? Of course not. Virginia aristocrats don't go to jail. Their fathers pay their shoplifting bills and keep it out of the paper."

The Senator remained quiet, staring at the report in front of her. She couldn't change the fact that an investigation showed the influential warden at a women's prison ran a brothel there and had caused the death of a young inmate who wouldn't go along with his scheme.

I tried again. "Nancy, the guards' depositions can't be ignored. What would they gain by lying?"

She looked at me again. "Annie, I can't take on this issue. I want to run for governor in two years. If I look like I'm coddling criminals, I might as well give up the notion right now."

"Senator, those women have been beaten and raped. One of them got killed. The warden sealed the coffin and said it was meningitis."

"So you say." Her smile was condescending. "Annie, these women are just different from you and me." Meaning they didn't have pedigrees that went back to Jamestown. "Why, the warden told me at my fundraiser last week that some of them are, you know."

"No, what?"

"Oh, don't play me that way. You know very well what I'm talking about." Her voice dropped to a whisper. "Some of them are lesbians."

"Lord, Nancy, you don't have to whisper the word, lesbian. The best families have them. Why do you think Aunt Margery nicked all those lace hankies? They certainly weren't for Uncle Powell."

The Senator rose and came from behind her desk. She whipped off her glasses and pointed at me with them. "I will not release that report to the press. Write me one that says my investigation could not substantiate the charges."

"How much did the warden contribute?"

"Do it."

"I can't."

"You won't."

"Let me hold the press conference. My name alone will draw a crowd of reporters. You don't have to be involved."

"Annie, the only way I'd let you do that is if you didn't work for me." The smile was pure bitch. "But we all know how badly you need a job."

* * *

When my brothers and male cousins ran the family business into the ground, and I refused to put my regional airline into hock to save their financial asses, the family name saved them from indictments. No judge wanted to have the Pearce name—one that had graced the annals of Virginia history for 250 years—stained in

18

that way. Why, that family had contributed so much to the Commonwealth, after all. A few, shady business deals could just be ignored, among gentlemen, of course.

Because I was related to the idiots—I wish I could attribute the idiocy to inbreeding, but it was just plain, simple bubba-ness—and because of some connection to the family business that to this day I still don't understand (the lawyers, who made out well indeed, do), the Bubbas' creditors took my company, too.

That made the papers for weeks. My aunts were appalled because my name was in the paper for something other than a debut, engagement, marriage, birth, or death. I found myself with no house, no business, no job, and little money. They only thing I had was that magic name, the one that opened doors otherwise locked to all except the privileged. That name got me the job with Senator Dale.

Now, that same name got me an appointment with the first, and so far only, African-American Governor of the Commonwealth of Virginia.

He motioned me to sit in an impressive leather chair across from his equally impressive mahogany desk. He gave me a gentle smile, one a father would give in indulgence to a child.

"You know, my family is originally from your part of Madison County," he said.

That told me he knew that my several times great-grandfather had owned his and that he also knew I was coming to ask him for help. If he relished the role reversal, he was enough of a Virginia gentleman not to bring it up.

He listened to me. He listened for a long time before he nodded.

"What can I do?"

I told him.

He did it.

* * *

When the proverbial dust settled, a warden lost her job and went to a prison of the maximum-security variety for manslaughter and pandering. The guards who had beaten a young mother to death for not prostituting herself joined the warden there. Several judges and state legislators had to resign when the warden's client book became public. A state senator who had tried to get me to change a damning report lost her bid to be nominated to run for governor.

19

The ordinary citizens of Virginia, so disdained by the old gentry, love honesty above all, and they do love to see the mighty fall. The state motto isn't *Sic Semper Tyrannis* for nothing.

The governor who exposed the whole sordid mess went on to be the first African-American U.S. Senator from Virginia. Oh, and I lost my job with the State Senator long before she lost her nomination bid.

But I still have my good name, except friends and the family I'm still burdened with now call me "Governor Pearce."

JUSTICE

The prosecutor stood and addressed the judge. "Your honor, there is only one witness to call for the sentencing portion of these proceedings."

The prosecutor turned toward the jury, let her eyes glisten with tears—you could show you were about to cry; you just couldn't go all the way—and said, "Kaitlin Haldane."

The bailiff intoned her name in a loud voice and summoned her to the stand. With a sigh, Kaitlin composed herself, a small hesitation just to collect her thoughts, but it was long enough for the prosecutor's head to whip around and scan the courtroom. The sympathy had left District Attorney Marcy Hogan's face—thank God the jury couldn't see—and her bright, blue eyes icily sought Kaitlin's.

Kaitlin stood, hands smoothing the lay of her suit. She had removed all her jewelry. Marcy had wanted her to wear them, all the beautiful gold and silver things Mitch had given her. This morning, when she stood before the mirror, Kaitlin had removed then one by one, placing them in a velvet-lined jewelry box, which she locked and put away in a deep corner of a closet.

Marcy had also told her to wear no make-up so she would appear bereft and weepy. "Gets a jury every time," she said. Kaitlin was bereft all right, but she had no more tears. Her make-up was immaculate.

21

Calm, with confidence, Kaitlin walked up the aisle, feeling the eyes on her, through the swinging gate, and to the witness stand.

The judge's eyes were kind when he looked at her. "Ms. Haldane?" She turned to him and looked him full in the face. He started to speak then stopped, taken back by the absolute serenity he saw. He cleared his throat and tried again. "Ms. Haldane, you are not under oath during this proceeding. As you know the defendant has been found guilty of murder in the first degree, and in the Commonwealth of Virginia, it is up to the jury to recommend sentence, either life in prison without parole or death by lethal injection. Before the jury arrives at its recommendation, which, by law, I cannot alter, any and all interested parties may address the court and comment on the sentence they deem appropriate. That is, you may tell us what sentence you would like to see the defendant receive. Do you understand?"

"Yes, of course."

Kaitlin turned to Marcy, though she could still see the faces of the jurors intent upon her, sending her sympathy. During the trial when Kaitlin testified, some had wept.

Kaitlin let her gaze drift to the defendant's table. The harried public defender scribbled notes, likely planning what he would say in summation instead of listening to the proceedings. Kaitlin continued to stare until the defendant met her eyes. Before he could bring his mask up, she saw he was scared to death. That was the subtle difference between him and his victim. Mitchell had looked him in the eye before the defendant shot him, and Mitchell had had no fear.

Marcy gave a slight clearing of her throat, and Kaitlin looked back to her. "Ms. Haldane," Marcy said. "I know this is difficult for you, but the jury would like to hear what you have to say about Mr. Roosevelt's sentencing. I'm not going to ask you any questions. I just want you to talk, to tell us what you want."

From the pointed look Marcy gave her, Kaitlin realized Marcy expected her say what they had rehearsed. Kaitlin turned to the jurors, supposedly the defendant's peers. A quick look told her none of them had grown up in The Berg, Alexandria's infamous public housing project where the defendant had lived his whole life.

"Some of this you've heard before," Kaitlin began. "Now, I want you to remember what's been lost here. Mitchell Sanders helped people. That was all he ever wanted to do. He was the best human being I've ever known, and never before had I been so deeply, truly, and sincerely loved. We had been together for eleven years, but that ended when Mr. Jamal Roosevelt shot him in the face."

She paused to let the words sink in, knowing they would remember the crime scene photos Kaitlin couldn't bear to see. The women jurors and a few of the men dabbed their eyes. "He fell on top of me. I had his blood and brains all over me."

Kaitlin again looked at Roosevelt. He stared at his hands atop the table. "Your honor, I'd like to approach Mr. Roosevelt." The judge's eyebrows climbed his forehead in surprise, and Marcy took a step toward Kaitlin, stopping only when Kaitlin raised a hand. "And I'd like to hold the murder weapon, item of evidence number 14A."

"What on earth for?" the judge asked.

The public defender was on his feet. "I object, Your Honor!"

Marcy recovered from Kaitlin's unexpected behavior. "We are not in proceedings here, Your Honor. Defense not only has no grounds for objection, there is no process for objection."

The judge rubbed his temples and sighed. "Attorneys, and Ms. Haldane, sidebar, please." The three gathered around the bench, and the judge addressed Marcy Hogan first. "Ms. Hogan, what do you know about this extraordinary request?"

Kaitlin spoke up. "She knows nothing about it, Your Honor. This is my doing. I'm a lawyer, and I've researched this. There is nothing which says I can't approach the defendant and that I can't see the evidence in a sentencing hearing. The evidence is here, because I know Ms. Hogan plans to brandish it during sentencing summation."

Marcy put a hand on a hip. "Look, Kaitlin, I'm the prosecutor here, and I don't know where this is going, except to unnecessarily prejudice the jury…"

"Ms. Hogan, I'm the judge here, and I'll decide where this is going."

The public defender got in on the action.

23

"I'm defense counsel here, and since I'm looking for grounds to appeal, I don't object to Ms. Haldane's approaching my client. But, no gun."

"I also want to ask him a question. One question," Kaitlin said.

All three responded at once. "What?"

Kaitlin leaned toward the public defender. "Look, your client has been convicted, but he gets to make his own plea for clemency."

The public defender reminded, "Prosecution gets the rebuttal."

Kaitlin turned to Marcy. "You got your conviction. You did a good job, and it's clean. There'll be no grounds for appeal, though I'm sure counsel will try. I'm the victim, remember? The person for whom we wrote all those victims' rights laws. Let me have a little satisfaction."

"Anything else we can do for you?" The judge's sarcasm was honed.

Kaitlin smiled at him. "I promise to recuse myself from any future proceedings you may preside over."

"You just bought yourself a judge." He looked first at the public defender then at Marcy Hogan. "Counselors, your objections are overruled. Return to your tables. Ms. Haldane, back to the witness stand." When everyone was in place, he addressed the jury. "Ms. Haldane may approach the defendant with the murder weapon, after the bailiff assures, once again, the weapon is rendered harmless."

* * *

Jamal Malcolm Roosevelt, his thug façade in place, turned to his attorney. "What's this? I don't want her talking to me. Ain't she done me enough harm?"

"And how much harm have you done her, you little bastard?" The attorney gripped Jamal's knee like a vise. "You sit here, you answer her question, and otherwise keep your cool. We'll get an appeal out of this."

Jamal stared at the floor. He had tried to say during the trial he had never wanted to rob the couple walking home from an evening in Old Town. The lawyer wouldn't let him say Sweetwater Eddie told him armed robbery was just an initiation, that if he didn't do it he had no balls, and that if the white folks gave him trouble, he should teach them a lesson. Jamal didn't know what to do next when the man showed him an empty wallet and told him he'd spent all his cash on dinner.

"Come on, man. The plastic," Jamal said. He waved the nickel-plated .45, but the two were so calm, much more than he was.

"I brought only cash with me," the man said. "Leave it alone, son."

"You ain't my father!" Jamal had never known his father, and he didn't like men, especially white men, calling him son. "All right, then. The bitch's purse." He had winced at that. Momma didn't like that word, didn't like it when his friends bandied it around.

"I didn't bring it." That was the same woman walking toward him now.

Jamal hadn't a clue what to do next. Eddie never said what happened if there was no money.

"What do you need money for?" the woman had asked him. "You're not on drugs. You're eyes are too clear. What do you need? Diapers? Food?"

No, no drugs. He'd seen too much to fall into that trap. The man had reached into the inside of his jacket. Oh Jesus, oh Jesus, he's got a gun! Jamal raised his arms to protect his face, forgetting the .45 was still in one hand. Jamal wouldn't know the man had reached for his business card—it was still in his fingers when the police bagged the body. The man ran a non-profit organization where Jamal could get food and other necessities.

In the moment, Jamal thought only of his mother, who had tried so hard, weeping at his funeral and wondering what she'd done wrong. That made Jamal tremble, and the gun fired. The man's face puckered as a curtain of stuff fanned out behind his head, showering the women who stood behind him. The man's body fell on her, and she was dazed, looking at the blood and brains all over her. She had looked up at Jamal, not seeing he'd pissed himself. Their eyes met, and what never came out in court were the words she said to him.

"Shoot me, too, so we can die together."

Jamal had dropped the gun and run.

He looked up at her, their positions reversed. She was the one holding the .45 now.

"Jamal, do you love anybody?" she asked him.

That confused him, but he couldn't stop himself from glancing over his right shoulder. Seated in the first row behind him was his mother, who held his two-year-old daughter, Jamalia. Jamalia's mother had died of a crack overdose when the child was four months old. Jamal had gotten custody. Well, his mother had, but he had intended to be the father he hadn't known. He just had really bad friends.

His lawyer had insisted Jamal's mother bring the little girl to court every day, and her presence in the courtroom had been the only thing in Jamal's favor. She was beautiful with her neatly braided hair, clipped with bright, little bows.

Each time he entered the court room, Jamalia had laughed, clapped her hands, and shouted, "Daddy!" She would reach for him, and it tore his heart not to be able to go to her and pick her up.

Jamal turned back to the woman. "I love my daughter more than anything in the world."

The woman lifted the gun, cocked the hammer, and pointed it at Jamalia. Even though everyone knew it wasn't loaded, there was a collective gasp. Jamalia's grandmother shrieked and tried to get her body between the gun and the child, and that made Jamalia begin to wail.

The judge slammed his gavel down and demanded order. The prosecutor put her face in her hands. Jamal's lawyer grinned.

Jamal started to get up, then stopped. He and the woman looked at each other. Jamal remembered again how the man's face had looked when the bullet hit him. He nodded to the woman and sat back down.

"I know, I know," she said.

He whispered his answer, but the woman nodded to show she heard him over the din. "I never meant for it to happen."

* * *

Kaitlin lowered her arm and forgave Jamal. She gave the gun back to the startled bailiff and walked to the rail of the jury box. The courtroom fell silent again, but several of the jury shrank back when she approached.

"Ladies and gentlemen," Kaitlin said. "Condemning this man to death is the easy way, isn't it? Gets one more animal off the street so he won't kill again. A simple, elegant solution, but what will it really do? Will it bring Mitch back? No. Will it bring me sleep at night? No. Mitch will still be dead, and I will still be without him, so what do we gain?

"Now, don't think retribution never entered my head. I was so angry at Jamal Roosevelt that I could insert the needle myself.

"Then, I remembered something Mitch lived his life by, something he and I believed in. No state, no government, no person has a right to kill. Government should be the example, and if the government kills, then, well, it's all right for you or me or Jamal to kill.

"You've heard me called a victim, and I was. I wallowed, then I got over it. If you decide to kill Jamal, you'll make me a victim again, especially if you think by killing him you're doing me a favor. Then, I'll always be a victim, and so will Jamal and his daughter. So will you.

"Jamal loves his daughter. I saw that. You saw that. But only I saw what was in his eyes when he shot Mitch, and it was fear, not hate. Today, Jamal got to feel what I felt, and that's enough for me.

"Let him think on what he did every day of a long life in the Greenville Correctional Facility. Let him explain why he's there every time his daughter comes to visit him.

"Thank you, and I apologize if I upset you. I ask you to consider what I've said, and I ask you to give Jamalia back her father."

Kaitlin Haldane walked past the glaring prosecutor and the shocked spectators. I kept the faith, Mitch, but you and Jamal made it hard.

Five hours later the jury returned from its deliberations, their faces unreadable.

The judge looked them over. "Ladies and gentlemen of the jury, what say you in this matter? Do you have a recommendation?"

The foreman stood. "Yes, Your honor."

WHEN GRAMMA CAME TO CALL

My grandmother came to visit today.

That's not particularly momentous unless you know that she's been dead for twenty years.

The doorbell rang, and when I opened the door, there she stood. She wore a pale lavender dress with a neat, folded hankie pinned over her left breast with an amethyst brooch. Her old-fashioned glasses with the rhinestones imbedded in the frames somehow managed to look good on her. Her fingernails were their usual formidable selves, painted bright red to match her lipstick. She looked dressed for church. In fact, this was exactly what she wore when we buried her.

"Hi, Doll!" She greeted me as if this were just a regular Saturday afternoon visit.

I was speechless."

"Are you going to stand there gawking? Come out here right now and give your grandmother a hug and a kiss."

I stayed in the doorway, my mouth agape. I didn't really want to "go" where she was, and I wasn't sure I wanted her in the house.

She smiled a familiar smile and spoke in her accustomed Irish brogue.

"Oh, no, dear. 'Twould really be unpleasant if I came in there."

I must be dead.

29

"No, you're not dead. I'm just here to talk over a few things, but it looks like I'm going to be doing all the talking."

I found my voice. "Gramma, you have to admit this is a bit, well, unusual."

"Well, of course it is! Dead people don't come to your door every day. At least I hope not. Margaret Elizabeth, I am not going to stand here on your doorstep for eternity—which I can do, you know—and wait for you to figure out what's going on." She pointed with one of those exquisite nails to a spot next to her. "Get out here, right now!"

I could never disregard that command tone. I had jumped to do its bidding often enough. When I stepped over the threshold, the yard, the house, the street were gone, and a whirlpool of color disrupted my equilibrium. I reeled with vertigo, then, a firm, living, flesh-warm hand gripped my arm.

"Don't look down," Gramma said. "You'll get used to it." I must have showed my doubt because I heard her tsk. "Goodness, girl, you fly airplanes, don't you? You're not going to let a little thing like this upset you."

"Are you here to take me into the light or something?"

"You're not dead. I already told you that, didn't I? I don't want to say it again. Now, go ahead and ask the other question."

All right, I thought, I'll play. "What are you doing here?"

"Oh, I just wanted to drop in and see how you were doing. It's been a while, you know."

"Why haven't you been here before?"

"You haven't needed me before."

"And I need you now?"

"Oh, is that how it is? You think you're too grown up to need your old grandmother's help."

"Look, if you've come all the way from wherever it is you came from to try the guilt trip, I am too grown up for that."

"Fine." She turned and started to walk away.

"Fine? That's it? Fine? You can't walk away from me like that!"

She turned, arms folded under her breasts. "And why not?"

"What the fuck is going on here?"

"I knew I shouldn't have come. You don't want my help. Stubborn, just like always."

She unpinned the hankie and dabbed at her eyes. This was a familiar scene, and it had a familiar effect.

"Gramma, I'm sorry. I'm just a little confused here."

She looked up at me, dry-eyed and smiling. "Ah! You've figured it out!"

"What? That I'm confused? You said it yourself. Dead people don't show up on the doorstep every day. Of course, I'm confused."

"That's why I'm here."

"You're here because I'm confused, but I'm confused because you're here. This is too complicated."

"Well, life was never meant to be simple. Or death, either."

"So, are you, well, in heaven?"

She sighed. "I'm where I'm happy. I wasn't truly happy until I died. One hell of a note."

"I always remembered you smiling."

"Through the pain, darling, but you know all about that."

Something fearful ran through me.

"Don't be afraid of it," she said. The tone was the same as when she soothed nightmares or skinned knees. "I'm no *bean si*. I'm here because you asked for me.

I closed my eyes and hoped when I opened them again she'd be gone.

"I'm still here, and so are you. You won't hide from this. I won't let you."

I opened my eyes. "What's that supposed to mean?"

"You have to deal with the unpleasantness."

That inexplicable fear came again, and my defenses came up. "I've dealt with plenty of unpleasantness."

"No, you push it aside or you joke or you make up excuses. You never look unpleasantness in the eye and tell it to go to hell."

"Look, this is enough. I'm scared. Take me home."

"You've always felt you had to survive at any cost. Give in to what you're trying to remember. It can't hurt you now."

* * *

I stood in a familiar yard. I looked down at myself. I was five years old and dressed in a pretty, print dress, lace-edged white anklet socks, and black patent leather shoes. Bruises, in various stages of fading, marked my arms and legs.

31

"Here it comes!"

I recognized the voice, and I didn't want to look.

My father, a young soldier, tossed me a beach ball, a consolation gift because at the last minute my mother wouldn't let me go on vacation with him. He and my mother were separated, and for weeks she'd declared how happy she'd be to have time to herself while I was gone. Then, she found out my father was also bringing a girlfriend, and that changed her mind.

So, I had decided to relive the day he came back from the beach. My mother dressed me up for that, but she dressed me up for everything then raged if those dresses got a speck of dirt.

As I contemplated why I was back here and now, the beach ball smacked me in the face—not hard, but it startled me enough that I fell. My father rushed over.

"Sorry, honey," he said. "Are you okay?"

I looked up into those wise eyes and wanted to tell him everything that was going to happen in the next forty years so he would know there was one thing I needed for him to change, but the five-year-old was in charge.

"I'm okay, Daddy. Is my dress dirty?" Going back inside with a smudged dress would not be good.

"No, baby. It's beautiful. Just like you."

When I realized I couldn't beg him not to kill himself, my tears came for real. He thought it was the usual tears whenever he had to leave.

"Don't cry, honey. You know I have to go even though I don't want to go." He set me on my feet and retrieved the ball. "Take good care of this, and we'll play again the next time I'm here."

He hugged me as if he didn't want to let go, and I didn't want that either. I smelled what I'd missed for so long—cigarettes, Old Spice, and a hint of bourbon. I watched him walk back to his car, and I wanted to run after him. The five year old stayed still as the car pulled away.

I didn't have to see to know my mother watched from a window. No sooner than Dad's car turned the corner, the door flew open and she pounded down the steps to the yard.

She stood over me, hands on hips, face in a scowl. "Some gift. Don't think you're going to bring it in the house. You'll break something with it."

She reached for it, and the five-year-old me didn't know any better. I moved it out of her reach.

The rage always came quickly but was slow to leave. She slapped the ball from my hands and grabbed me by the arm. The blows came fast and hard. One thing I had learned back then was to go limp, not fight back. It was over sooner that way.

When she let me go, I looked for my ball, but my mother found it first. She held it up out of my reach and took a bobby pin from her hair. She jabbed the ball over and over until there was no hope of repairing it, then she threw it in my face.

"There! Play with that!"

I would never learn to let go of things. I should have attached no emotion to my dolls, my toys, my books. Had I done that, I wouldn't have hurt so bad each time she took her rage at my father out on the things I loved. I couldn't bear to remember what she did to the puppies my dog had.

The next time my father came, I told him the bruises on top of bruises came from my falling out of a swing. I told him, too, that I had "busted" the ball. That didn't matter to him. All my failings never mattered. Whenever he hugged me and called me his best girl, everything was perfect.

* * *

I was back beside my grandmother, but the child me came along. She looked up at me with tears in her eyes.

"I'm sorry," was all I could say.

"Can't you do better than that?" my grandmother asked.

With the same anger my mother felt I turned on her. "She was your daughter! You made her that way!"

She lifted her hands in triumph, her eyes raised to the non-existent sky. "At last!"

"I hated her. And I loved her. All I ever wanted was to understand why it had to be me. Why did she have to take it out on me?"

"Because I taught her the only lesson I could. Survive at any cost. That was all a woman could do in my day. All that anger, my anger, her father's anger, all added up and dumped on you. Every bruise on you was one on my heart. And I never said a word."

"We never told anyone." The insight that had eluded me for years was now so obvious. "We tried to survive by being quiet."

My grandmother nodded, and she smiled. "But no more."

"No more."

How simple it was to face this at last and let it go. I felt so light, so weightless, I began to float.

"In her own way, she loved you," I heard Gramma say.

I remembered when I cleaned out the house after my mother died I found a box with all the silly things I made for her in school, all the cards bought by others with my name scrawled in them. That she had saved them was a shock.

"I know," I said.

Gramma clasped her hands in front of her chest, as if praying. "Now, this circle is broken."

I began to rise, slowly at first, then faster. I looked down. The little girl held my grandmother's hand. They both smiled and waved.

My grandmother brought a hand to her mouth and shouted, "May the road rise to meet you!"

That was always the last thing she said when she left to go home.

"And may you be in heaven an hour before the devil knows you're dead!"

I heard her laugh. "I was, darling, I was!"

I rose until they were specks, then, in a wink, they were gone, and I grew lighter and lighter as I rose. How, I wondered, will I get down?

"Why come down at all?" came my grandmother's whisper.

Why, indeed.

I soared.

THE LAST TUSKEGEE AIRMAN

The blond, blue-eyed news anchor furrowed his brow, set his jaw, and fixed the camera with a no-nonsense expression.

"Woody Broadwater died of complications from advanced age at the State Mental Hospital today."

He shifted to the next camera. "Broadwater made quite a fuss years ago when he claimed he and other niggers had flown combat missions in the Great Heroic War, the conflict the defunct United Nations called World War II. Let's go to Daniel Young, live, at State Hospital. Daniel?"

The screen filled with a head and shoulders shot of a crew-cut young man whose pancake make-up couldn't hope to disguise the pimples. It did nothing to cover the tattoo across his forehead— "BERSERKER!" Over his shoulder, just out of focus, was a gray, stone building with barred windows and a crumbling façade.

"Thanks, Roger," Daniel said. "Woody Broadwater was committed to State Hospital in 2010 after he made repeated, unsubstantiated claims that nigger pilots—the so-called Tuskegee Airmen—flew sophisticated aircraft in what Liberal scum call World War II. In spite of his evangelical persuasiveness, especially among people of diminished intelligence like him, this network, with the assistance of the Young Historians of Cobb County, debunked his claims. Just as we've done for other claims of so-

35

called…" His disdain came through the television set. "…civil rights activists."

"Yes, Daniel, we have some tape. Can we see that, please?"

File footage of Broadwater from a decade before filled the screen. The aging man was debating a shaved-head, brown-shirted Young Historian who shouted and jabbed an angry finger at the reed-thin black man. The on-site reporter provided voice-over.

"This was the scene in Alabama several years ago when Broadwater, obviously senile, stood on the steps of the Heflin Courthouse claiming it was the site of the alleged airfield where the Tuskegee Institute had supposedly trained niggers to fly airplanes. The Tuskegee Institute and other discriminatory nigger colleges have subsequently been closed as a requirement of the White Race Redemption Act."

The file footage switched to show some grainy, fading photographs, and the narration continued.

"Broadwater based his entire argument on faked photos such as these, which had been housed in the old National Air and Space Museum, closed after patriots boycotted that liberal stronghold for its revisionist stand on the Holy Bombing of Jap Cities.

"Photo experts from the Young Historians were able to show that Broadwater's ridiculous claims were part of a conspiracy by niggers, feminazis, Jews, and other sub-human races to unseat Christian White Men from their God-given place in society and government. Counter-culturists had taken real photos of white pilots and superimposed nigger heads on them."

Next came a courtroom scene, where a dazed Broadwater, his face swollen and bruised, listened as a judge declared him "one crazy nigger" and confined him to a mental institution for life.

Young continued, "Broadwater proved to be a contentious patient here at the State Hospital. He incited the crazies by telling them they had right and privileges they clearly did not have under the Revised Constitution of 2013. He was disciplined numerous times, including just last week for refusing to take his behavior modification medication. Broadwater's spurious claims opened a long-healed wound in the White American psyche, a wound caused by agitators and liberals who tried to rewrite history and God's laws."

The anchor interjected himself back into the report. "That's right, Daniel. It boggles the mind how such revisionist crap can come before a God-fearing public, doesn't it?"

"Well, this was before the Controlled Speech Amendment was passed."

Roger smiled and nodded. "Ah, yes, the mend for a lot of ills."

"Yes, it finally put a stop to any platform for counter-culturist views. The scary thing is these liberals had actually reached into the Holy Sanctuary of the War Department itself and altered records to make it look like these supposed nigger pilots had been able to fly airplanes and that they accomplished some mission or other."

"Hard to believe in this day and age that someone would give credence to a crazy old darkie."

"Well, the niggers were always so easily controlled by the counter-culture for its own traitorous ends. Broadwater did attract a lot of attention, but in the face of unrelenting scrutiny by The Speaker, everyone could see the truth."

"The Speaker came out of retirement to head off that affront to White History, didn't he?"

Young smiled and nodded. "Well, you can retire the warhorse, but he still has some kick, Roger."

"That he does. Thanks for that thorough report, Daniel. White Power!"

"White Power, Roger."

Roger turned back to the main camera.

"Coming up after the break, the State Church adds a much-needed tenth prayer interval for the schools. Sports. And film of the most recent public execution of an unwed mother and her bastard."

* * *

In the Mississippi National Ghetto, a twelve year old girl, her brown skin as clean as her mother could get it with rags and spit, turned off the antique iPod to conserve its aging battery. She pulled open a drawer on a wooden chest and reached inside.

With a care most twelve year olds wouldn't use, she removed a cloth patch, its colors faded, its inscription barely readable. Even though she couldn't read—there were laws against her kind going

37

to school—she knew what it said. Her great-grandfather had taught it to her like a mantra: 99th Fighter Squadron–Tuskegee Airmen.

In Newthistory such a squadron, such a name didn't exist. History had been revised so it no longer conflicted with what "the people" wanted. A wave in 2010 became a tsunami, but the only history the girl knew was from her great-grandfather. Though his time in her life was brief, those reminiscences brought it to life for her.

She reached into the drawer again and drew out a plastic model of an ancient warplane called a Mustang. The silver paint had chipped and peeled in places, but its red tail, the trademark of the Tuskegee Airmen, still shined.

Her great-grandfather told her many planes like this one had streaked the skies over the Mediterranean Sea and southern Europe during World War II. The pilots were men whose skin was the same color as hers. No school would teach this, no one could talk about it on pain of imprisonment.

Her mother always got so nervous and weepy when the girl took the forbidden items out in the daylight. Someone might turn them in to the Ghetto Police.

The girl glanced up at the small, street-level window. It was summer, so her mother had taken down the cardboard cover for fresh air and light. Today, the girl could see a patch of bright, blue sky. Sometimes she had even seen a real airplane high in that sky, a tiny speck against the blue. Whenever that happened, she would whisper, like a prayer, "Some day, I fly a plane, too."

She climbed atop some boxes so she could lean her arms on the sill. She held the model plane up against the sky. Its silver paint seemed brighter, the red tail more crimson.

The distant planes she saw from that window were silent in their passage, but in her head the girl knew the plane this model represented made a loud noise.

The Mustang shouted its defiance at its enemies—"them mezzershits and fukkers" her great-grandfather would say. When he talked about those days, his old eyes would sparkle, and the girl could see he was far away in his mind, in another time and place, a better place.

The girl swooped the model back and forth across the square of sky and made low, growling, engine noises. With her other hand, she started a dogfight with imaginary enemy planes whose pilots had white skin and blue eyes.

This game she never tired of, and in her mind she sat in the Mustang's cockpit. She moved the controls whose names her great-grandfather taught her. Yoke, rudder, aileron. He also taught her lift, thrust, weight, drag. Pitch, roll, and yaw were her prayers. Immelman, half Cuban eight, loop.

As the Mustang chased its enemy to ground, the girl's lips puckered around the imitated sounds of long-silenced guns that spat a hellfire of bullets until the enemy plane dived in a plume of smoke and flame then crashed.

And the daughter of the grandson of the last Tuskegee Airman did a victory roll above the Mississippi National Ghetto and flew where hate would never touch her.

o;-)
ANGEL

The creator-hacker sat at her cosmic computer and said, "Interactive."

"Which world?" the computer droned.

"Sol system, third planet."

The computer gave a mechanical sigh. "That one again?"

"Look, it's my world."

"Yes, you still keep trying to get it right."

"It was my first creation, all right. I mean, not everybody's first world is perfect."

"Yes, but really, how many wars are we up to now?"

"Are you going to open the file or not?"

The computer took on an indignant tone. "You're the creator-hacker. You've given me a command. Of course I'll open the file. Do you want to start in the beginning or at the last string of code you entered?"

"I don't want to re-live the past five billion years. When did I enter the last string?"

"About two millennia ago. The computer giggled as it reviewed directories and subdirectories in the file. "Oh my. You know that one called the Galilean?"

"Yes?"

"You interacted with him."

"Yes?"

"Well, you won't believe what he's told everyone."

* * *

The systems engineer regarded the creator-hacker before him.

"Generally, when we create worlds, we monitor them more than once in a couple of millennia their time."

"I made so many corrections in the code," the creator-hacker said. "I thought this last one would do it."

"There was interaction."

"I'm not the only one who's done that."

"It was certainly innovative to give the physical beings different genders, I must say."

"Well, we're different genders. I made them in our image, and it was only two. That was the only way to accomplish replication."

During the silence a galaxy died, several million stars were born, and 4,263 sentient species in the universe became extinct.

"I would think," the engineer said, "that you'd be insulted that after all the millions of years you've spent on these beings, they've decided to make their deity male."

"Yes, well, I really didn't realize that these two different genders would find so much to disagree about. A third one just seemed, well, superfluous."

Another galaxy came into being, a few million stars nova'ed, and 5,728 pre-sentient species crawled from primordial ooze and walked on land before the systems engineer spoke again.

"This is a real mess. I don't see how you can de-bug the program. I'm for a wipe."

The creator-hacker's fractals now flashed and expanded exponentially.

"We can't do that. There is so much promise in this program. Yes, some code is bad, but the base code is magnificent." She brought her fractals under control. "Of course, I am biased."

"I agree the base code is elegant, but there's no virus protection. Worms abound. In short, and in the vernacular of some of the subroutines, it's fucked up."

The creator-hacker considered for several millennia before posing an impertinent question. "Did you ever think that we're just lines in something else's code?"

"No chance. I've been around a long time. I've looked in every back door and gateway, through every firewall there is. What's your point?"

"Well, what if we were created by someone like me and someone hit the delete key?"

A universe emerged from a black hole, expanded to its limit, imploded, then exploded again before the systems engineer replied.

"If we don't wipe, what do you propose to do about it?"

"Leave it alone?"

"Unprecedented."

The systems engineer called up the program of the Sol system's third planet.

He read the code line by line. "This is amateurish in places."

"It was my first creation."

"Oh, don't be so defensive. Everybody has a first, and everybody has trashed their first creation. But, I can understand your attachment to it and its heuristic physical creations."

He extended sympathetic fractals toward her. They touched hers and merged.

"You may not have to wipe. They are well on their way to deleting themselves."

Their fractals separated, and they both sighed.

The creator-hacker mustered her resolve.

"I guess I should tell you I, uh, wrote freedom of choice into the code."

"What? You trusted a heuristic program with freedom of choice combined with sentience? Who was your original systems engineer to let you do that?"

"Uh, you were."

"I was?"

"Yes.

"Well..."

"I'm entirely responsible, of course."

"No question about that." The system engineer's fractals contracted as he pondered.

"Look," the creator-hacker said, "I'll turn my remaining projects over to other creator-hackers. Let me devote all my time to fix this."

"You're already too attached. If you concentrate on that one world, you'll be over-involved. Besides, no one has ever done that before, either."

"Isn't it about time?"

Millennia went by as pulse-beats.

The systems engineer examined the status of the creator-hacker's other programs. She'd learned something. All the others were pristine, exquisite, orderly.

"You do understand that once you embark on this course, you won't be able to create any new worlds?"

"I understand."

Her fractals flared in sadness. Her ideas for new worlds would never take on life in the cosmic processor. Yet, she could see how lines of code from those ideas could be melded into her first creation to improve it.

The systems engineer saw the direction in which her fractals moved. "That might work."

This intrigued him. The physical beings inhabiting her program were sentient, just beginning to suspect their real origin. A few had even plugged in to the 'Net and seen what cyberspace really was. They now lived in worlds in their own heads, the pallor of their skin made paler by the light from computer monitors glaring in the dark. They would waste away until cyberspace absorbed their electrons, mixed them with star stuff, and shot them to new corners of other universes.

The engineer sighed. This one had always been the creator-hacker with the most promise, and the taste of her fractals left him sated for eons. She was just unorthodox in her programming.

"Very well. Turn your projects over to the others and assume responsibility for—what do you call it?"

"Earth."

"Where did you come up with a name like that? No, never mind. Just take over 'earth' full time."

"As usual, you are wise."

"I'm the wisest cyperpunk you know."

Their fractals merged for the last time.

* * *

"Game over. Play again?"

The adolescent cybergod smiled. His brilliant game-play had saved the world yet again. He had accumulated plenty of energy points and a few extra lives. He adjusted his glasses, held together with a cosmic string, and gnawed a fingernail.

"Play again?" the computer repeated.

"Yes."

His fingers flew over the keyboard.

* * *

The creator-hacker sat at her cosmic computer and said, "Interactive."

"Which world?" the computer droned.

"Sol system, third planet."

The computer gave a mechanical sigh. "That one again?"

"Look, it's my world."

"Yes, you still keep trying to get it right."

THE END

ABOUT THE AUTHOR

Phyllis Anne Duncan is a retired bureaucrat but one with an overactive imagination—at least that's what she's been told since she first started making up stories in elementary school prompted by her weekly list of spelling words. A commercial pilot and former FAA safety official, she lives and writes in the beautiful Shenandoah Valley of Virginia. A graduate of Madison College (now James Madison University), she has degrees in history and political science. Her love of politics continues to this day.

She is the First Vice President of the Virginia Writers Club, one of the oldest writer organizations in the country.

Her fiction has appeared in numerous literary journals and anthologies. When not writing, reading, reviewing books, singing in a UU choir, watching the New York Yankees, or cheering on Dale Earnhardt, Jr., she delights in spoiling her grandchildren.

SOCIAL MEDIA

Twitter: @unspywriter
Facebook Author Page:
https://www.facebook.com/unspywriter/
Blog: www.unexpectedpaths.com (available as a Kindle subscription)
Instagram: paduncan1
Amazon Author Page: http://bit.ly/PADuncan (links to all published works)

ALSO BY THE AUTHOR

Short Story and Flash Fiction Collections

Rarely Well-Behaved, 2000 (out of print)
Blood Vengeance, 2012
Fences and Other Stories, 2012
Spy Flash, 2012
Spy Flash II, coming soon
The Better Spy, 2015 (a novel in stories)

Novellas

My Noble Enemy, 2015
The Yellow Scarf, 2015

Short Story Singles

"Spymaster," 2016
"Blood Cover," 2016
"Best Served Cold," 2016
"Brave New World," 2016

Novels

A War of Deception, coming in 2017